DannyPettry.Com, LLC
An Independent Publisher
Beckley, West Virginia

Monsters Are So Much Fun

Published by:
DannyPettry.Com , LLC, Beckley, West Virginia 25801. USA.
DannyPettry.Com provides educational resources and materials for
independent learners.

Online: http://www.DannyPettry.com

Library Publication Data

Pettry II, Danny W.
    Monsters Are So Much Fun.

Danny W. Pettry II

ISBN: **978-1470196059**
EAN-13:   **1470196050**

Book cover designed by *KillerCovers*.

Children's Book.

Printed in the United States of America.

Photo and Picture Credits are on p. 28.

ALySSa
Zoe
Gage
& HaLey

Best Wishes in life!
From Danny

Toy Monsters featured in this book
are created and copyrighted by:

Der Bears Toy Factory
© 2012

MONSTERS ARE SO MUCH FUN!

Count them.

Monsters are so much fun.

Add them up.

Tell me the sum.

1

O-N-E.
One.

I believe
you are having fun.

Count them.

Monsters are so much fun.

Add them up.

Tell me the sum.

2

T-W-O
Two.

I believe
you know what to do.

Count them.

Monsters are so much fun.

Add them up.

Tell me the sum.

3

T-H-R-E-E
Three.

I believe
you have eyes that see.

Count them.

Monsters are so much fun.

Add them up.

Tell me the sum.

F-O-U-R
Four.

I believe
you want to play more.

Count them.

Monsters are so much fun.

Add them up.

Tell me the sum.

F-I-V-E
Five.

I believe
you're having a jive.

Count them.

Monsters are so much fun.

Add them up.

Tell me the sum.

6

S-I-X
Six.

I believe
it's a monster mix.

Count them.

Monsters are so much fun.

Add them up.

Tell me the sum.

7

S-E-V-E-N
Seven.

I believe
you can count to seven.

Count them.

Monsters are so much fun.

Add them up.

Tell me the sum.

8

E-I-G-H-T
Eight.

I believe
this game is great.

Count them.

Monsters are so much fun.

Add them up.

Tell me the sum.

N-I-N-E
Nine.

I believe
you will be just fine.

Count them.

Monsters are so much fun.

Add them up.

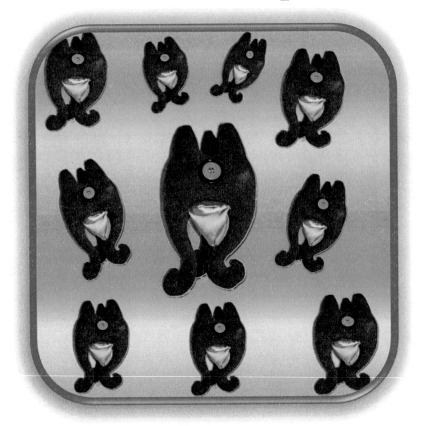

Tell me the sum.

10

T-E-N
Ten.

I believe
you want to read this book
again.

Monsters Are So Much Fun!

10
9
8
7
6
5
4
3
2
1

ACKNOWLedgeMeNtS

Special Thanks to the good people at kickstarter.com and the many wonderful people who pledged support for the monster book project!

Largest Monsters
Derric Capteina and Maile Johnson

Larger Monsters
Charles Dixon, Alicia Gonzales, Denise Clark, Owen Walker, Michelle A Howell, Jennifer Paul, and Tj Hopson

Large Monsters
Lisa M Lorelli, Tammy Mollohan, Gail Stoll Patton, Stacie Scott, Rebecca Minor, Melanie Daniels, Frank and Megan Constantino, Charles Clements, Christopher Stoddard, and (Jimmy, Emily, Gage, and Zoe Pettry), and Jeremy and Erica Lively

Small Monsters:
Rachelle Williams and Amanda Brenwalt

Smaller Monsters: Anne Stewart
Smallest Monsters: Ryan Stockstad

PHoto CredItS

Derric (Der) Capteina

Derric Capteina is the owner of *Der Bears Toy Factory*.

He creates his toys out of love. He lives in New York City amongst his many sketches and creations.

He loves Rocky Road Ice Cream, house plants, and loose fitting T-shirts.

DaNNy PeTTry II

Danny Pettry works as a Recreational Therapist for children.

He loves coffee and conversation. He also loves reading dystopian novels.

His favorite food is cookies. His nephew calls him "uncle cookie."

He lives in West Virginia.

Get Issue # 2

Get Issue # 3

COMING IN 2013

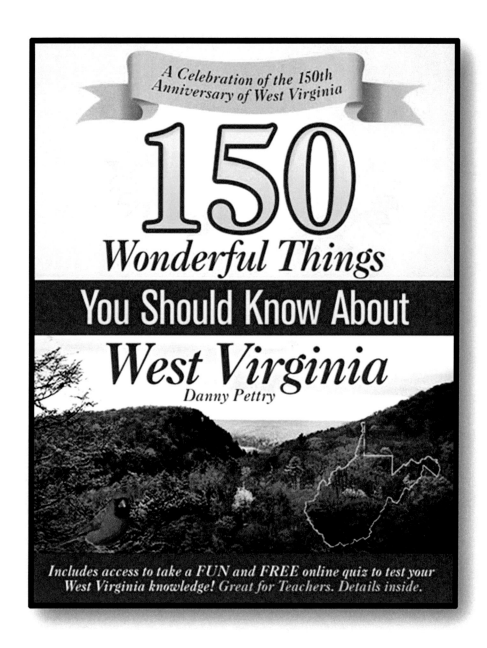

A Celebration of the 150th Anniversary of West Virginia

150

Wonderful Things

You Should Know About

West Virginia

Danny Pettry

Includes access to take a FUN and FREE online quiz to test your West Virginia knowledge! Great for Teachers. Details inside.

Made in the USA
San Bernardino, CA
25 October 2017